A Snake on the Moon

By Annie Sweet
Illustrated by P. Srigley

WigglesWorth Press & SrigleyArts.com

Library and Archives Canada Cataloguing in Publication:
Please contact the publisher for this information

ISBN 9780988008120

Layout by WigglesWorth Press
Cover design by Patricia Srigley
Cover art by Patricia Srigley

Published by:
WigglesWorth Press & SrigleyArts.com
Montreal, Quebec, Canada

Additional Titles by the Author

A Snake in the Paint
A Snake in the Cake
Halloween on the Farm
The Dream Team: On the Farm
Kitty Cat Catnap
Stomp, Stomp, Stomp: The Elephants' Lunch
Very Merry Mousemas

Wiggles the Snake was playing at the park
Sliding on the slide until the sky got dark
Swinging on the swing until Mister Moon
Rose overhead like a bright orange balloon

Mister Moon looked down at Wiggles and said,
"Little snake, it is time to go home to bed."
All around Mister Moon, the stars twinkled bright
They twinkled and sang, "Goodnight, goodnight, goodnight."

Wiggles said, "Goodnight," and waved his striped tail
He shook off sand and picked up his sandpail

Wiggles slithered down the path into the trees
That ringed the park and creaked in the breeze
The path was so dark, he couldn't see
The tip of his tail or his one snake knee
Wiggles got so scared, he turned tail and fled
Back to the park instead of his cozy bed

The moon's glow bathed the park in faint light
But moon had closed his eyes for the night
He was snoring, wearing his nightcap
Cuddling his teddy bear in his moon lap
The stars slept too, dreaming sweet dreams
Of cheesy ice-cream made from moonbeams

Wiggles was only a tiny little snake
He began to quiver, shiver and shake
He was scared all alone at the park
Surrounded by creaking trees and the dark
He wanted to go home to his cozy bed
But the black forest filled him with dread

Wiggles hissed, "Wake up, wake up, Mister Moon!"
The moon yawned. "Is it morning so soon?"
"It is not the morning yet," Wiggles said.
"It's night and I want to go home to bed,
But the path is too dark, and I can't see
All the scary things that there might be."

The moon said, "I'll lend you my teddy bear."
Wiggles said, "That is kind of you to share,
But how about a moonbeam instead,
To light the way to my cozy bed?"
For a little snake, Wiggles was pretty smart
Even though he wasn't so brave in his heart

The moon said, "My beams aren't bright like the sun,
They aren't bright enough to get the job done."
Mister Moon was sad, he heaved a big sigh
Wiggles was sad too, he started to cry

"Wait, I have an idea," the moon said
"I know how to get you home to your bed!"
The moon's idea made him smile so big
He turned a somersault and danced a jig
He woke up five stars and juggled them about
"Yippee! Again, again!" the stars did shout

"How will you get me home to my bed?"
Wiggles asked the moon, so high overhead

"Why, I will give you a ride. How about that?"
And moon pulled a long string from under his hat.

Wiggles really wanted to visit the moon
So he said, "I like that idea. Can I go soon?"

Mister Moon dropped one end of the string
Tied in a loop, like a lasso swing
Wiggles climbed on and he began to rise
He rose so high, he couldn't believe his eyes
He rose past the trees, clouds and stars in turn
Stars so bright, he almost got a sunburn

He reached Mister Moon and climbed on his chin
Right below Mister Moon's mile-wide grin
"Hold on," Moon said and raced across the sky
Wiggles held on, and in the blink of an eye
He was looking way down from outer space
On his very own little home-sweet-home place

Wiggles said, "Thank you, thank you for the ride."
And down, down, down, the long string he did slide.

When he touched down, he gave a goodnight hiss
And blew Mister Moon a big goodnight kiss

"Goodnight," the moon said. "Goodnight and sleep tight."
And Wiggles did sleep tight in his bed all night.

Additional Titles by the Author

A Snake in the Paint
A Snake in the Cake
Halloween on the Farm
The Dream Team: On the Farm
Kitty Cat Catnap
Stomp, Stomp, Stomp: The Elephants' Lunch
Very Merry Mousemas

Made in the USA
Las Vegas, NV
10 June 2023

73242655R00017